Now You See Them, Now You Don't
Supernatural Tales

by

Harrison Powers

Watermill Press

Contents of this edition copyright © 1982 by Watermill
Press, Mahwah, New Jersey

Printed in the United States of America

Illustrations by Jim Odbert

ISBN 0-89375-700-4

Contents

Contents

The Whiz Kid

Keith Young never talked about anything but history. Even Mr. Wallace thought it was unusual. Not that there's anything wrong with liking history. I like history myself and I do well in it. So I know what I'm talking about. But Keith was not your average history student.

His specialty was local history. By local, I mean all of New York City. He knew everything that happened along Kings Highway during the Battle of Long Island. He knew who built the old farmhouse at Twenty-third Street. He could tell you how Sheepshead Bay got its name. He even knew when Coney Island stopped being an island.

Mr. Wallace was a good history teacher. Yet even he didn't know all that stuff. More than once, Keith would say, "Check it out, Mr. Wallace." And Mr. Wallace would go to the library to check this fact or that. I think he wanted to catch Keith in a mistake just once. He never could. Keith was one of those guys who was always right.

What got Mr. Wallace most was that every time he went to the library, there was Keith. He would always be sitting in the same place, too. There was this big picture of the Brooklyn Bridge. It was an old photo, taken when the bridge first opened. Keith always sat at a table under the picture.

"Don't you ever go outdoors?" Mr.

*Keith always sat at a table under
the picture.*

Wallace asked him once.

Keith was very polite. "Oh yes, sir," he said. "I walk a lot. People used to walk a lot in the old days. Not everybody had a horse, you know. Most people couldn't afford to keep one. So they walked."

"Yeah, I know," Mr. Wallace said.

I think that's when he gave up on Keith. There wasn't anything you could say to the guy without getting a history lesson in return.

Mr. Wallace gave Keith an A+ on all his tests and papers. Just between you and me, I don't think Mr. Wallace ever read them. I think he just put down A+ and let it go at that.

But once, Keith returned a test to Mr. Wallace.

"Excuse me, sir," he said. "You gave me an A+."

"So?" Mr. Wallace asked. "Isn't that good enough?"

"It's not that," Keith said. "I made a mistake. I don't deserve an A+."

Mr. Wallace looked worried. He hadn't really read the test. He had just marked it A+, as usual.

"Show me the mistake, Keith. Sorry I missed it."

"Here, in question five. You asked me about the Battle of Trenton. I said it was December 25th, 1776. It wasn't. It was December 26th. Washington crossed the Delaware on Christmas Day. He didn't fight until the next day. I forgot."

"Oh," Mr. Wallace said. "You're right. Let me change your grade." He took the paper and erased the plus sign from the A. "There. Is that better?" he asked.

"Thank you," Keith said. And he left.

Can you believe it?

Well, one day Keith left his gloves in class. Everyone had left except Mr. Wallace and me. Mr. Wallace was just going out of the room when he saw the gloves.

9

"You're right. Let me change your grade."

"George," he said. "You go by the library on your way home, don't you?"

Naturally I said yes, because I do.

"It's pretty cold today," Mr. Wallace said. "And it looks like Keith left his gloves. Why don't you stop at the library and give them to him?"

"Sure, Mr. Wallace," I said. "You think he'll be there?"

Mr. Wallace sighed. "He's always there. You'll find him by the old picture of the Brooklyn Bridge."

"Sure, Mr. Wallace," I said.

Actually, I had known where Keith would be. I just wanted to see the look on Mr. Wallace's face when he said it.

It was a cold day, so I ran most of the way. When I got to the library, I was out of breath. And I was a bit dizzy — the way you get sometimes from running. Only I must have been dizzier than I thought.

When I got to where Keith always sits, I saw something I really didn't see. I *thought* I saw Keith climb up on the

11

*Then I thought I saw him climb into
the picture.*

table. Then I thought I saw him climb *into* the picture of the Brooklyn Bridge.

I knew I was seeing things, of course. So I closed my eyes and shook my head. That seemed to clear things up. Next time I looked, Keith wasn't there. His books were on the table, though. So I figured he was in the bathroom. Or, maybe he was looking for a book.

I went over and put the gloves down beside his books. Then I looked at the picture. Now, I know this didn't happen. I shouldn't even tell you. But I thought I saw something move in the picture. I looked very closely.

What I thought I saw, but I didn't, of course, was a guy getting on a trolley car. And he rode across the Brooklyn Bridge to New York.

I've always wanted to ask Keith about it. But I never did see him again.

The Angel of Briggs Street

It was a "depressed" neighborhood. That's what the mayor called it the last time he visited. The streets were dirty. Many buildings were empty and boarded up. The others were badly in need of repair.

All the streets were the same—all except Briggs Street, that is. On Briggs Street, there were families living in all the houses. Flowers grew in

On Briggs Street, the buildings were clean and freshly painted.

window boxes. The buildings were clean and freshly painted. And, perhaps what you noticed most, there wasn't a scrap of litter anywhere.

This was easy to explain. Essie Briggs saw to it that every scrap was picked up. Every morning, she went on "litter patrol" with her shopping bag. Many of the kids on the block went with her. "We must keep my street clean," she would tell them. It was a joke on the block that the street must have been named after her.

Essie loved flowers and plants. That's why all the houses on the street had them. Whenever anyone had a birthday, she would give a pot of ivy. Other times, she'd give pink mums or a bunch of daisies. She got a lot of kids started on window-box herb gardens. She showed them how to make Christmas presents with what they grew.

There was one vacant lot on Briggs Street. It was where Number 122 should have been. Folks say the house burned down years ago. Essie used the lot to grow her flowers and herbs.

For some reason, houses with flowers growing outside get fixed up in other ways, too. A house with a flower garden just doesn't get left unpainted, for example. So people on Briggs Street did a lot of fixing up.

"I've always had flowers and nice things on my street," Essie would say. "I guess I always will."

They had some trees, too. At one time, the city had wanted to take the trees down and build a parking lot. But Essie saved them. When they came with a bulldozer, Essie was sitting under the first tree. She wouldn't move. By the time the police came, a crowd had gathered. Somebody called the newspaper. Even a TV truck came. Essie was on the six o'clock news.

The mayor happened to be running for Congress at the time. So he came down to get on TV, too. The trees stayed.

Essie was on the six o'clock news.

The whole area had a high crime rate—all except Briggs Street, that is. A woman was robbed once a few years back. So Essie talked to Nat Freed about it. She told him nicely that he should look after people on the block. Nat was big enough to do it. He was embarrassed, but he said okay, he would try.

Nat asked Rose Lucas to watch during the day when he went to work. And Rose asked other people to watch when she had to go shopping. Pretty soon, a lot of people were watching out for other people. Anybody looking for trouble just naturally went someplace else.

The funny thing about Essie was that no one was sure where she lived. She always had an excuse if someone wanted to visit. "Oh, my place is a mess," she would say. Or, "Maybe another day, honey."

If someone asked her straight out where she lived, she would wave her hand. "Oh, just down there," she would say. People got the idea she didn't want visitors. So they just stopped asking.

Big cities are full of unusual people. So no one thought Essie was strange or anything. She just overdid the gag about it being *her* street.

It would have ended there if it wasn't for the census. Dori Gibbs was hired as a census-taker. Since she lived on Briggs Street, she thought it would be easy to count the folks living there. It was. Only she couldn't find Essie.

It was funny because Essie was always around. But when Dori went looking for her, Essie would disappear.

Then, early one morning, Dori spotted Essie on litter patrol. "Essie, wait up," she called.

Essie excused herself. "Just a minute, dear. There's a bottle in the alley I must get."

Essie never came out of the alley. Dori checked the houses on both sides.

Whenever she asked, people would

reply, "Essie? No, Essie doesn't live here. She lives down the street somewhere."

Dori suddenly had a creepy feeling about Essie. She decided to do some checking. First, she went to City Hall. She found some old town records. And the more she dug into the history of the neighborhood, the more interested she became.

At one time, a Briggs family owned a huge farm along the river. It included what was now Briggs Street. The street must have been named for that family.

In 1880, there were three Briggs families on the street. Over the years, they all moved away. The last of them left in 1910. In that family, there was an Esther Mary Briggs—age 14. "Essie!" Dori said to herself. "Maybe it *was* her street."

When Dori came home that night, Essie was coming out of the vacant lot where she grew her flowers. Dori quietly walked up to her.

"Essie?"

"Yes, dear?"

"Please, Essie, may I ask you some questions?"

"I'd be happy to stay and chat," Essie said. "But you'll have to excuse me a moment, I . . ."

"No you don't," said Dori. And she took hold of Essie's hand. "Not till I've asked you one thing."

Essie looked frightened. "Please," she said. "You're hurting my hand."

Dori felt the stone of Essie's ring. It was pressing into Dori's hand. It hurt, but she had to find out.

"Are you Esther Mary Briggs?"

"No, no! Just Essie. I'm Essie. Everyone knows that."

It may just have been the light, but Dori thought Essie was fading away.

"Well, where do you live?"

"Over there." Essie waved her free hand.

Dori thought she could see right through Essie now.

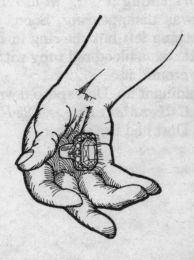

Soon, there was nothing left but the ring in Dori's hand.

"Where? What number?" she demanded.

Essie's voice was fading, too. "One —two—two," she said. *That was the number of the empty lot!*

Dori thought she would faint. Essie was disappearing. Soon, there was nothing left but the ring in Dori's hand. It was a blood-red ruby with diamonds around it.

Holding it up, Dori spotted writing inside: *Esther Mary Briggs, 122 Briggs Street.* Dori had her answer.

The Sacred Oath

At first, Jake thought it was just a rusty piece of junk. But as he turned it over, he realized it was a sword. The tip was gone and the blade was chipped. Rust had eaten at the handle. But it *was* a sword handle—a hilt. Jake could have sworn to that. And it fit nicely into his hand. And there was a crossbar.

Jake sat for a while and studied his find. *What a terrific discovery it was!*

He wondered how old the sword was. Who had used it last? He felt the weight of it. Then he waved it over his head and shouted, "Charge!"

A man, hurrying through the park, looked up. He gave Jake a funny look. Jake felt a bit foolish being caught playing soldier.

He figured he had better take the sword home. Maybe Artie or Biff would have some ideas about it.

They had some ideas all right. Biff figured it was a Viking sword. "See, it's just plain iron," he said. "Really old."

"Maybe the leather or cloth on the hilt rotted away," suggested Art.

"Maybe," Jake agreed. "I don't think there were any Vikings around here, though. We're too far from the ocean. Let's get it cleaned up and show it to Pops."

"Pops" was their foster father, Stan Fisher. The three boys were all about the same age. And they had all come to live with Stan at about the

"Charge!"

same time. They thought of themselves as brothers, even though they weren't at all related. In fact, none of them had any idea who their parents were. They had started calling Stan "Pops" when they were small. The name just stuck.

The sword didn't look too bad when they got the rust off it. Jake shaped a new point on it, and Biff wrapped the hilt with a leather shoelace.

Pops was interested. "It's at least Civil War," he said. "Maybe older." He turned it over in his hands. "Look, there's a maker's mark on the blade. It looks like an H in a circle. Why don't you see if you can find out something about it in the library?"

The three boys agreed that was a good idea. They hurried off to the library where Mrs. Eden helped them find books about old weapons. After two hours of looking, they made a discovery. A sword-maker, named Hartz, had used an H in a circle as his mark. Hartz died in 1802. So now they knew the sword was made before that.

"And look," Jake said. "It says he once made swords for a Major Wendell King. Major King led a company of soldiers from this town – Preston. They fought with George Washington at Valley Forge."

Biff knew what was coming. His brothers were going to kid him now because his name was the same as the Major. Biff was only a nickname. His *real* name was Wendell King.

"Hey, *Major* King." Art poked his brother. "May I touch your sword?"

"Aw, come on, Artie." Biff poked him back. "Do you know how many people there are named King? There must be thousands—maybe millions. And there have got to be plenty of Wendells among them."

"He's just kidding, Biff. Forget it," Jake said. "But it sure would be funny if the Major turned out to be related to you somehow."

"I have a great idea," Artie said.

"None of us know our blood relatives. Let's take a blood oath on the sword. We'll mix our blood like they did in the old days. Then we can at least *say* we're blood brothers."

"Where should we do it?" Biff wanted to know.

"It's got to be someplace private," suggested Jake.

"The churchyard," Artie said, "the old burial ground. I know a place where nobody can see us from the street."

"The churchyard it is," said Biff. "Okay with you, Jake?"

"Sure. How about tomorrow after school?" Jake took the sword from his belt and placed it on the table. "A blood oath it is!"

"Outside with that thing," Mrs. Eden shouted at them, "before someone gets hurt."

*　　　*　　　*　　　*

The next day, the boys found a quiet spot behind a gravestone. They sat on the ground in a circle. The sword was in the middle. Each boy pricked a finger on the point of the sword. Then they clasped hands.

"Blood to blood," said Jake.

"Brother to brother," answered Biff.

"Forever!" Artie finished the oath.

The boys sat in silence. It was Jake who spoke first.

"Biff," he asked, "how did you know what to say?"

"I don't know," said Biff. "It just came. It sort of seemed right. How about you?"

"Same with me," Jake said. "I had a feeling."

Artie didn't say anything. He got up and walked around the cemetery, stopping to read some of the gravestones. Suddenly, he stopped and called to the others.

"Biff! Jake! Come quick!"

The two boys came running. Artie pointed to a tall granite stone. "I've found him! I've found him!" was all he could say.

In large letters, at the top of the marker, was the name Major Wendell King. Then Artie pointed to faded writing farther down the stone. The three boys stared. They couldn't believe what they saw. There were two more names.

"Corporal Jacob Smith. Oh no, that's me," Jake whispered.

The last name was Private Arthur Long — Artie. They were all there. But that wasn't all. At the very bottom of the stone was this:

"Blood to blood,
Brother to brother,
Forever."

Died at Valley Forge, 1778

A small boy was playing just outside the churchyard. He watched as three men walked through the gate.

Three men walked through the gate.

They were dressed in ragged old uniforms — blue and white with large brass buttons. Their legs and feet were wrapped in rags. Two of the men carried old muskets. One wore a sword. The little boy stared at them. But he must have looked away for a second. When he looked again, the three soldiers had vanished.

A Strange Voyage

"Hello."

Lee was startled. No one ever came out on the old dock. That's why she liked to go there—to be alone. Now here was this strange girl. Lee hadn't seen her coming.

"Hi," Lee answered.

The other girl didn't speak again. So finally Lee said, "I'm Lee Forest. You come out here often?"

Lee hadn't seen her coming.

"Oh, yes," the girl replied. "I come every day. I like to look out at the harbor and watch the ships."

Lee thought it was funny that she had never seen the girl before. But then she thought, "Oh well, I guess we get here at different times."

There was something strange about the girl. Lee tried to figure out what it was. She seemed nice enough. She spoke a little formally maybe. And her dress was a little old-fashioned, but kind of cute. Lee gave it up. "People are certainly allowed to be different," she thought. Then she said out loud:

"I like to watch ships, too."

The girl didn't say anything.

"In fact, I sail a little myself," Lee added.

The girl seemed interested at this.

"Yeah. My friend Walter has a small sailboat," continued Lee. "We just fool around in the harbor, though. It's too small to take out on the ocean."

Now the girl actually seemed excited. "Would it be okay," she asked, "if I come with you sometime?"

"Sure," Lee said. "Walt's nice. He won't mind. How about tomorrow?"

"Oh, that would be so nice of you," the girl said. "You can pick me up right here if your friend doesn't mind."

"Sure. We'll sail Walt's rig right up to the dock. Is three o'clock okay?"

"Oh, thank you!" Suddenly, the girl kissed Lee, and then she ran down the dock.

"Hey," Lee called after her. "What's your name?"

"Victoria," the girl called back. And then she was gone.

*   *   *   *

Victoria was waiting when Lee and Walt slipped alongside the old dock.

"Climb down," Lee called up to her.

Victoria, still in her old-fashioned dress, climbed down the ladder. With great care, she settled herself in the front of the boat. Walt caught the wind, and they were off.

There was a good stiff breeze, so it wasn't long before they came upon the entrance to the harbor.

"We'd better start back," Walt called. "With this wind, the waves must be three or four feet high out on the ocean. That's too much for this craft."

Lee called to Victoria, "Watch out for the boom as we turn around." And then Lee ducked, waiting for the long pole to swing by. But it never swung. And Victoria hadn't moved.

"Something's wrong," Walt said. "The rudder's stuck. I can't steer."

"Let the sail go free," Lee called.

"I tried," Walt hollered back. "The pulleys are jammed."

"I'll drop the sail," Lee said. "Then we can row back."

But nothing would budge. The sail was set and the rudder was locked. The small boat flew across the water, straight through the harbor entrance and out into the ocean. Victoria just sat calmly looking out to sea.

Lee moved back to help Walt with the rudder. Nothing would move it. The waves pounded against the bottom of the boat and splashed over the sides. The wind was howling.

"The reef!" Lee shouted over the wind. "We're headed straight for the rocks. We'll be killed!"

Then they noticed that Victoria was standing in the front of the boat. *She was calling to someone.*

"Randall!" she cried. "Randall, I'm coming."

Without warning, she slipped over the side of the boat—straight into the water. A large wave swept over her and...she was gone.

Lee screamed. Then, almost at once, the wind died, and the waves calmed down. The ocean became as smooth as glass. The rudder of the boat worked, and the pulleys for the sails came unstuck.

Lee and Walt sat huddled together

She was calling to someone.

in the bottom of the boat. They were too frightened to move. When they got their breath back, they began to search for Victoria. They spent an hour rowing back and forth along the reef. But she was nowhere.

Finally, they decided they had better head back into the harbor. The Coast Guard must be told.

*   *   *   *

Captain Beckwith promised to send a boat out to the reef.

"We haven't had any trouble out there in forty years," he said. "During World War II, a Navy patrol boat went down when it hit the rocks. I remember a local girl had a boyfriend who died in the accident. It made her kind of crazy. Poor thing. She must be almost sixty now. If she's still alive, that is. *She tried to kill herself by sailing out to the reef.*"

The Old Rolltop Desk

It was just an old rolltop desk. You know, the kind that has a cover that rolls down to close it. Mrs. Elkins had bought it in an antique shop. It was to be a surprise for Mr. Elkins' birthday.

But Mrs. Elkins' son, Bobby, had a feeling there was something funny about that desk. It smelled funny, for one thing. Mrs. Elkins said antiques

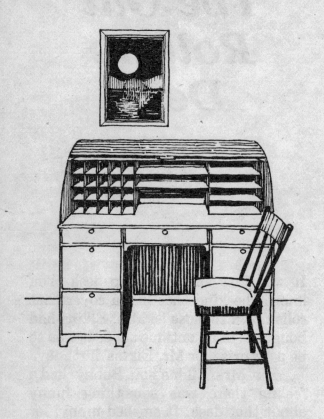

It was just an old rolltop desk.

always smell. That's true, but this wasn't an old smell. It was more like a burnt smell.

Mr. Elkins was a salesman who worked out of his home. He was away on a trip when the desk was delivered. That's the way Mrs. Elkins planned the surprise. When he got home, it would just be there. A rolltop desk was something he had always wanted.

Right after it was delivered to the house, Bobby started poking around in the drawers. After all, that's what you do with an old desk. You always think maybe somebody left something in it. Well, first Bobby noticed this burnt smell. But that wasn't all. The drawers stuck.

"So what?" you might say. "So the drawers stuck. Drawers in old desks always stick."

That wasn't the way it was, though. The drawers opened easily enough. What Bobby noticed was how they closed. When you pushed on them,

45

it felt like something was pushing back.

Bobby took a drawer all the way out. Then he looked into the hole. Nothing. So he put the drawer back. And he pushed it closed. Something pushed back. The drawer actually reopened itself after he had closed it.

Bobby told his mother. "Oh, for heaven's sake, Bobby," she said. "You and your imagination!" Of course, this is what Bobby *thought* his mother would say.

"Anyhow," Mrs. Elkins said, "I don't want you playing with the desk. And your father doesn't want you fooling around in his office."

Mrs. Elkins figured the best way to keep Bobby out was to lock the office. So that's what she did. And that should have been the end of it. But it wasn't.

Bobby had a lively curiosity. He hated questions without answers. A drawer that opens by itself is a question. Perhaps the store where the desk came from had an answer.

*Bobby hoped the store would
have the answer.*

The store owner was an old guy. He was small, wrinkled, and had wispy gray hair. Bobby introduced himself. "My mother just bought an old rolltop desk from you," he said.

"So?" the old man said. "What's wrong with it?"

"Oh, nothing's wrong with it," Bobby said. He didn't want to explain about the drawers that opened by themselves. "I was just wondering if you know where it came from?"

"Of course I do," the man snapped. "I know all about all my stuff. It came out of the old Harlan Falls Mill."

"But the Harlan Falls Mill burned down," Bobby said.

"Of course it did," said the man. "Now run along, kid. I'm busy."

Bobby wasn't quite satisfied. "Is that why the desk smells burnt?" he asked.

"I suppose so," the man said. "It's a good desk though. Nothin' wrong with it."

"It's just that I thought everything burned up in the fire—that there was nothing left," Bobby said.

"Well, the desk didn't burn up. It was saved."

"Do you know whose desk it was?"

"Yup."

"Whose?"

"Old man Greene. He was the company bookkeeper for forty years. He wouldn't quit. Wouldn't give up the desk, either. They say when the fire broke out, he wouldn't leave the desk."

"Did they drag him away?"

"Nope."

"Then what happened?"

"Old man Greene burned up in the fire."

"You mean he died?" Bobby asked.

"That's what usually happens when you burn up." The old man thought this was pretty funny. He laughed. Actually, it was more like a cackle than a laugh. "Now run along, kid. Go on—scoot."

"But...," Bobby began.

"I said, *scoot!*" That seemed to be that.

What Bobby wondered was how Mr. Greene was burned up but the desk wasn't. "Well," he thought to himself, "I guess it just wasn't." Still wondering, he went home.

His father had just arrived when Bobby got there. Mr. Elkins was hugging his wife. "Have I got a surprise for you!" she said to her husband. "Just wait. It's down in your office." She led the way downstairs. Mr. Elkins followed. And Bobby followed him.

Mrs. Elkins took the key out of her pocket and unlocked the door. "The snoop here couldn't keep out of the surprise," she said. "So I locked the door."

They all went into the office. "Well," Mr. Elkins said. "Where's the surprise?" He was smiling the way people do when they expect something good to happen. Mrs. Elkins looked around. The desk was gone.

"Where...," she stammered. "There

The desk was gone.

was a desk... I bought you the desk you admired... the old rolltop. It was right here. And now it isn't!"

But there *was* something there. And they all saw it. Where the desk had stood, *there was a pile of black ashes.*

What Ever Happened to Cora Brown?

Cora Brown put on her shawl. "Today," she said to herself, "I think I'd like to be a dog."

One second, Cora was there. The next second, she wasn't. In her place was a rather grand-looking collie. It trotted off down the street. Cora's shawl lay on the ground.

In her place was a rather grand-looking collie.

It wasn't a magic trick. Speaking plainly, Cora was a witch. She got her power from her shawl.

An old friend had given the shawl to Cora for her fifth birthday. The woman died shortly after. Her name had been Cora, too. The family called her Aunt Cora.

Cora's mother put the shawl away for her daughter. She waited till Cora turned thirteen before she took it out again.

The shawl was beautiful. It was made of Irish linen and trimmed with lace. Tassels hung from the edges. No one knew how old it was.

Aunt Cora had said it was given to *her* when *she* was five. It was her duty, she said, to pass it on.

So Cora's mother had put it away. After much pleading, Cora was allowed to wear it when she was thirteen. It was to be worn only for special times.

Cora's mother didn't know about the power of the shawl. Cora had discovered it herself quite by accident. Her mother wasn't home. With nothing better to do, Cora went to the cedar chest and took out the shawl. Putting it on carefully, she admired herself in the mirror.

"I am a rich Spanish lady," she said playfully.

Instantly, she was ten years older! She had flowing black hair down to her waist. Diamonds sparkled at her ears. Three rings flashed on her fingers. Her long gown was satin.

She was frightened that first time. She shouted, "No, no! I'm Cora Brown." And, instantly, she was.

It took a little doing for Cora to get used to her power. And she thought it best not to tell her mother.

Trouble began when she started changing herself into animals. And, eventually, she got careless about locking her door.

One day, Cora's mother noticed a sea gull on the lawn. "Strange," she thought. "It must have lost its way. There's not much water around here."

Cora's shawl was lying on the lawn. Her mother picked it up and put it away.

"That's no way to treat such a beautiful shawl!" her mother shouted at her later. She was very angry.

In science, her class had been talking about flying. Cora thought she would like to try it out. So, she had become a sea gull. But, of course, she couldn't tell her mother that.

Another time, Cora's mother saw a monkey scampering down the side of the house. She ran to Cora's room. The shawl was on the bed. The window was open. Cora was gone.

She hollered at Cora about the shawl again. But that wasn't what she was worried about anymore. She was beginning to feel frightened.

Finally, one day, she found a Siamese cat curled up on Cora's bed. Cora was supposed to be in her room doing homework. Now Cora wasn't there. The shawl was in a lump next to the cat.

Mrs. Brown shooed the cat out of the house. She didn't like cats. Then, about an hour later, Cora rang the doorbell.

"I forgot my key," she said.

"Where have you been?" her mother asked.

"Oh, just out for a breath of air," Cora lied.

"With no coat? Not even a sweater? It's cold out!"

"I wasn't cold."

"What was that cat doing in your room?"

"What cat?" Cora knew she was in trouble.

"Don't *what cat* me, Cora Brown. There was a Siamese cat in your room. And your good shawl was in a lump on the bed."

"That was just Pru, mother. It's Angie's cat. I was taking care of it.

Angie's at a pajama party overnight. And her parents aren't home either. Now you've chased it out! What'll I tell Angie?" Cora was giving it all she had. Pretending to be upset, she ran to her room.

Mrs. Brown called Angie's mother. "Hi, Agnes. Say, is Angie home?"

"Sure. You want to talk to her?"

"Yes. I just wanted to ask her about her cat."

"Angie doesn't have a cat."

"Oh. Well, never mind then. I had a problem with a cat and I thought it was Angie's. Sorry—my mistake."

Mrs. Brown hung up. She wondered what to do. She thought she had better talk to her husband about it.

"Tom?" she said to her husband. "You remember Aunt Cora?"

"Sure," he said. "Your old friend who gave Cora the shawl."

"Yes. What did you think of her?"

"Okay, I guess. Maybe a little funny. I remember once I had to chase a pig out of her living room. I had gone next door for something and she wasn't home. I heard this oinking and squealing." He laughed. "I never did find out how that pig got in her living room."

Mrs. Brown was *really* worried now. She wasn't sure how to tell her husband. So she came right out with it.

"Tom, I think Aunt Cora was a witch. I think there's magic in that shawl. And now, I think our Cora's a witch." And she told Tom all she had seen and found out.

"I don't believe it," cried Mr. Brown. "It just can't be true!" But he was worried. They decided to keep a close watch on Cora, just to be sure.

That's why Mrs. Brown was watching the day Cora turned into a dog. It *had* to be the shawl, she decided.

And that's why, with her husband watching, Mrs. Brown picked up the shawl. She lit a fire in the fireplace. Then she threw in the shawl.

Cora was in her room at the time.

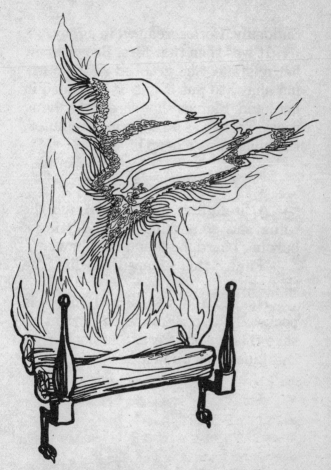

Mrs. Brown threw the shawl into the fire.

Suddenly, Cora screamed in agony.

It was then that Mrs. Brown knew her mistake. She grabbed at the burning shawl to put it out. It exploded in her hand. Flames shot across the living room. There was no chance. In minutes, the house was a heap of ashes.

*　　*　　*　　*

A firefighter, poking through the ruins, saw something white. Lifting a burning board, he found the shawl.

"Funny this escaped the fire," he thought.

He stuffed the shawl into his pocket. "Maybe Frances will want to save this for our Cora. She's only five. But kids grow up fast."

Night Train

Charlie listened to the moan of the train whistle.

"*Wha-a-a-w, wha-a-a-w, whaw, whaw.*"

The train was coming to the crossing at Depot Road. Charlie checked his watch—8:35 P.M. The train was right on time.

Charlie liked the sound of a train whistle at night. "We have to have night sounds," he would say. "It would be too quiet without them—spooky quiet."

But, maybe he liked train whistles because he was from an old railroad family. And he worked for the railroad himself. He was freight manager for all of north Georgia. His home was in Barnwell, halfway between Rome and Atlanta.

Both Charlie's father and grandfather had been engineers. And his great-grandfather had driven the last train on the Rome-to-Atlanta run when General Sherman invaded Georgia. That was in 1864, during the Civil War. Great-grandpa was only 28 then, with a new bride at home in Barnwell. The train was a wood-burner, brand-new. And it could do 75 miles an hour. Folks called it "Old Hundred" because that was the number painted on it.

The trouble was, Union troops cut the tracks at Barnwell. They tore up steel and built a roadblock eight feet

Charlie's great-grandfather had driven the last train on the Rome-to-Atlanta run.

high. But great-grandpa wouldn't stop. The train blew up. They never did find anybody alive.

Charlie Bates thought about his great-grandpa as he lay awake listening. He had been surprised when Asa Cadwell complained about the noise made by a midnight freight.

"It shrieks like a crazy thing," she had said. "And it wakes me up every night."

"But, Miss Cadwell," Charlie had replied. "There isn't any midnight freight through here. The last train at night is 8:35."

"Are you trying to tell me I'm hearing things, Charlie Bates?"

"No, ma'am. I'm just saying there is no train after 8:35."

"Well, suppose you just stay up and listen sometime." She shook a finger under Charlie's nose. "Maybe you'll find out something about your own railroad."

"Crazy old woman," Charlie said to

himself. But he decided to stay up and listen anyway.

Sure enough, just at midnight, he heard it. And it wasn't the *wha-a-a-w, wha-a-a-w* of a modern air horn. It was the high shriek of an old steam whistle.

Suddenly, his blood ran cold. He heard three short blasts — a distress signal! From the sound of it, it was coming up on Depot Road.

Charlie pulled on a jacket and ran for his car. Racing through town, he made it to the tracks in less than a minute. He was just in time to see the last car of a train vanish into the darkness. And, just for a split second, he thought he saw the number 100 on its side.

"Crazy," he said. "Completely crazy."

The next day, he called Atlanta.

"Bud," he asked the stationmaster, "what have you got that comes through here at midnight?"

There was a pause at the other end. "Nothing, Charlie. You know that. The freight goes through at 8:35. Then there's nothing till morning."

"Well, something went through last night," Charlie said. "An old steamer."

"What?" Bud started to laugh. "What've you been drinking, Charlie?"

"Very funny," Charlie said. And he hung up. Then he dialed the Chief of Police.

"Al, Charlie Bates here. You get any complaints about train whistles lately?"

"Yeah," the chief said. "Matter of fact, I have. I was going to call you. Asa Cadwell complained, and then Frank Wills."

"Well, how about coming down to the tracks with me tonight? At Depot Road. Make it a quarter-to-twelve. I'd like to find out what's going on."

"Sure, Charlie. See you tonight."

*   *   *   *

Chief Al Hucks was waiting when Charlie pulled up. Charlie parked behind Al and got into the squad car.

"Roll down the window, Al, so we can hear."

"What's going on, Charlie?"

"I don't know, Chief. Maybe we'll find out." Charlie didn't mention what he thought he had seen the night before.

It was two minutes before midnight when they heard it—three short shrieks and then three more. Distress signal!

"Al!" Charlie pointed down the tracks away from the sound of the train. "Shine your light down there."

The chief put on his spotlight. About 200 yards down, the tracks were torn up. There was a pile of logs and rails where tracks should have been. A big bonfire blazed. Men with guns stood on both sides.

The train shrieked again. Its headlamp lit up the crossing.

"We have to stop her!" Al shouted.

"Too late," Charlie hollered back.

As the speeding train crossed Depot Road, the two men saw its number. There could be no mistake. It was Old Hundred. The whistle screamed once more. Then the train hit the roadblock.

There was the screeching and crashing of wood and steel. Then it blew up. Al and Charlie dove into a ditch as huge chunks of wood and iron flew by. And they stayed in the ditch for the rest of the night.

With the first light of dawn, they carefully looked out. The tracks ran free and clear as far as the eye could see. There were no men with guns. And there was no wreck. The roadblock was gone.

The early morning freight rumbled through. The crew waved from the cab.

"What do you suppose we saw last night?" Al scratched his head.

"I'm not sure, Chief," said Charlie. "But just between you and me, I think

It was Old Hundred.

what we saw was my great-granddaddy going to glory."

"That's crazy, Charlie. Old Hundred blew up in 1864."

"I know that," Charlie said. "So I'm going to let *you* explain to Asa Cadwell about that train she's been hearing."

At Home with a Ghost

When the Parks family arrived at their new house, Vincent was waiting for them.

"Welcome," Vincent said. "You'll love it here."

"Thanks," said Sam. "I'm Sam Parks. This is my wife Laura. And this is my son Mike."

"So nice to meet you. I'm Vincent."

"Hi, Vincent. Where do you live?"

"Here," Vincent said.

"Oh. You mean next door," Sam said.

"No, here," Vincent said. He could see the Parks didn't understand. So he said, "Come on, I'll show you." And he led the way upstairs.

The house was empty except for one room. This was the room Laura had planned to use as a sewing room. Only now it had a bed in it. There was a dresser, a desk, and a chair. The walls were covered with pictures. The room was neat and clean.

"Wait a minute," Laura said. "You mean you moved in here? We don't even know you!"

"Yes you do," Vincent said. "I told you. I'm Vincent."

"Vincent who?" Sam wanted to know.

"Just Vincent." He sat down on the bed. "Like it?" he asked. "Those are the

74

school colors. Mike and I will be in eleventh grade together at Lincoln."

"You play football?" Mike asked.

"Sure. If you want me to," Vincent said.

"I'm going to try out for defensive back," Mike said. "What do you play?"

"Anything you want," Vincent said. "I'm not fussy."

"What do you mean what *I* want? What about the coach?"

"Oh, he won't care," said Vincent. "I do pretty much as I please."

"You're pretty sure of yourself," said Mike. "I've got to see this."

"Now, wait a minute, you guys," Sam said. "First things first. Vincent is not living here! That's final! He wasn't invited, and we don't even know who he is."

"I keep telling you. I'm Vincent."

"That does it," Sam said. "I'm calling the police."

"No, don't do that," Vincent said. "You'll just feel like a sap later."

"Don't call me names, kid." Sam was getting hot now. "You will leave on your own legs or the cops will drag you out!"

*　　*　　*　　*

When the police came, Sam told them the problem. Then he led them upstairs. When he opened the door to Vincent's room, Vincent was gone. The furniture was gone. The walls were bare.

"Seems like he left," said the sergeant.

"Yeah," Sam said. "I guess so. Sorry to bother you."

"No problem," the sergeant said. "Sometimes runaway kids move into an empty house. They see us coming and scram. Happens all the time."

"Yeah, I guess so," Sam said. "Thanks."

"Don't mention it." The police called in on their radio and drove off.

*　　*　　*　　*

76

Moving in was going smoothly. "Where do you want this chair, lady?" one of the movers asked.

"Upstairs in the middle room," Laura called.

"No room," the man said. "It's full."

"Oh no," Laura groaned. Then she called, "Sam... I think we've got trouble."

They went upstairs to the middle room. There was Vincent with all his things as before.

"Maybe I should explain," said Vincent.

"Please do," Sam said.

"I'm a ghost. I have orders from headquarters to live here. You don't argue with those guys. You just do what they say."

"Now look," Sam said. "Don't kid me. I don't —"

"I know," said Vincent. "You don't believe in ghosts. Okay, let me show you. Promise you won't scream or faint or anything?"

The Parks family looked at one

another and promised.

Vincent floated two feet off the ground. Then he turned upside down in midair. Then he disappeared. A mist filled the room. "That's me," Vincent called from nowhere. Pictures spun on the wall. The bed bounced up and down.

Then Vincent reappeared. "Okay?" he asked cheerfully.

Sam had his mouth open and couldn't shut it. Laura sat down on the bed. Mike gave a long whistle.

When they all recovered, they agreed Vincent would stay. He promised he wouldn't be any trouble.

Actually, Vincent was quite helpful. He insisted on doing the dishes. After each meal, the dishes would sail gently to the sink. The water turned on by itself. When they were washed, the dishes hung from the ceiling till they dried. Then they stacked themselves in the closet.

At school, Vincent decided Mike should play quarterback. "It's better

Then he turned upside down in midair.

for your image," he told Mike. "I'll play right end and catch anything you throw."

He did, too. Lincoln High never had such a winning streak. They'll never forget the time Mike was sacked, and the ball popped loose. It flew straight up about 40 feet. It made a right-angle turn, wobbled another 40 feet, and dropped into Vincent's arms. Touchdown!

The Parks family became very fond of Vincent.

"He's like a brother," Mike said.

"Yes, I know," said Laura. "He's a fine boy."

"A fine boy," Sam agreed. "Or — *whatever* he is."

Vincent stayed for a year. Then, one evening, he came down with his suitcase.

"Got to go," he said. "Orders from headquarters. Some family is moving in over in Northfield. They're kind of nervous about it, like you were. I'm

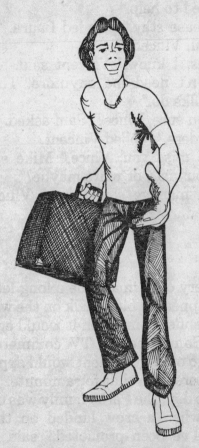

"I've got to go," he said.

supposed to help."

"Please stay," pleaded Laura. "We love you, Vincent."

"Yes, I know," Vincent said. "But you don't need me anymore. These other folks do."

"You sure, Vince?" Sam asked.

"Orders," replied Vincent.

"I'll miss you, Vince," Mike said. "Can you visit, or write maybe?"

"I'll manage something," Vincent promised.

*   *   *   *

Every once in a while a long letter would appear in blue chalk on the walls of Vincent's room. Then it would erase itself. Sometimes, a TV commercial would go off and Vincent would appear on the screen to chat for a minute.

One day, the Parks family was on a picnic when a crow landed on their table. "I've been promoted," said the crow. It was Vincent!

A crow landed on their picnic table.

"I'm going to headquarters." He reached his beak into the basket and pulled out a sandwich. "I won't be in touch anymore."

"Good luck, Vince," Sam said.

"We're happy you're a success, Vincent," Laura said.

"Take care," said Mike. "Thanks for being a buddy."

"Sure," Vincent said.

The crow flew off. They watched him fly up about 2,000 feet. And then he disappeared. They never saw Vincent again.

Corry Wales

Corry Wales wouldn't have noticed the cold air if the weather hadn't been so hot. It was mid-July. Corry had been at the beach. And now she was on her way home. She took her favorite short cut — through the cemetery. Every once in a while, she would feel a spot of cold air.

That's funny, she thought. *There*

are no trees and no shade. Still, it's cold. Brrr . . . . . She hugged herself to get warm. Then, a little further on, the air was just as warm as before.

"Freaky," she said. Then she forgot all about it. She figured it had something to do with air currents.

The next time she felt the cold air was in August. This time, she was at her great-aunt's funeral. Corry had never been to a funeral before, but her mother felt she should go.

Corry stood waiting to put a single rose on the coffin. *That's kind of nice,* she thought. Her aunt really loved roses.

But as she put down her rose, she felt the coldness again. There was no breeze. The air was just suddenly icy. Corry shivered.

"Why, what's the matter, Corry?" her mother asked.

"I don't know," Corry answered. "It's just . . . suddenly I feel as cold as

. . . as death."

"Hush," her mother said. "This is no place to make bad jokes like that. You're just upset. That often happens the first time you attend a funeral."

Corry thought her mother was probably right. And it did sound like a bad joke.

The summer heat lasted well into September. And it was on a day early in that month that Corry had the feeling once again. She was on her paper route late in the afternoon.

Corry delivered a paper to Mrs. Spector. There was a thermometer on the porch, so Corry stopped to look. "Whew! Ninety-five degrees in September," she sighed as she drew her hand across her wet forehead.

"Hot, isn't it?" Mrs. Spector had come out to get her paper. And that's when Corry felt cold. She shivered.

"What's the matter, honey? Are you sick?" Mrs. Spector asked. "Sit

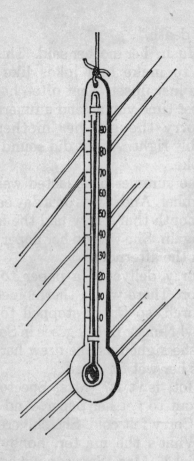

There was a thermometer on the porch,
so Corry stopped to look.

down on the porch a minute. I'll get you something to drink."

Corry didn't feel well. She was so cold. So she did as she was told. She sat and watched as Mrs. Spector went into the house. Mrs. Spector was young— thirty maybe. And she was pretty.

The cold spell seemed to pass quickly. Corry felt warm again. But, as she sat waiting for her drink, something bothered her. She thought back to the other times she had felt so cold.

She thought of the time in the cemetery. Then she thought of her aunt's funeral. *Maybe it was air currents. Or, maybe it was just nerves like Ma said.* But this time, just as she got sick, she had noticed something else. What was it? Corry tried to remember.

"Whew, it's hot," she said again. And she looked at the thermometer. It still read 95 degrees. That was just what it said before.

"The thermometer! That's it! That's what was wrong!" Corry remembered that the moment Mrs. Spector came to get her paper, the thermometer had dropped to 40 degrees. Now Corry was scared.

No, she said to herself. *It's not possible. I'm sick, that's all. I'd better get home.* She got up to leave just as Mrs. Spector returned with something to drink.

And once again, Corry felt the deadly chill. This time she took a good hard look at the thermometer. Sure enough, it read 40 degrees! Corry wasn't imagining. And she wasn't sick.

"Thanks, Mrs. Spector. I . . . I don't think I need a drink," Corry stammered. "I have to go."

"No you don't, honey," Mrs. Spector purred. "You can stay with me. You feel cold again, don't you? Just like I do. I'm always cold now. Don't worry. You'll get used to it." She put down the glasses and reached a hand out to Corry.

Corry backed away. "I've got to go," she said. "I have papers to deliver." She took the porch steps in one bound. Her bike fell. As she struggled to pick it up, she saw Mrs. Spector coming. The air was getting colder.

I've got to get away. I've got to get warm. This was all Corry could think.

Finally, she was on her bike and moving. An icy hand reached for her. But it slipped and let go, and Corry sped away.

She arrived home drenched in sweat.

"Good heavens, girl," her mother scolded. "Do you have to ride like a crazy person in this weather? You're all overheated. Go take a cool shower."

"No thanks, Ma. I think I like being hot." She handed her mother a news-paper and started up to her room.

She was halfway up the stairs when

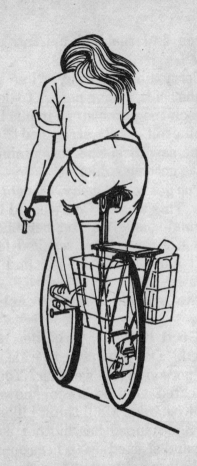

Finally, Corry was on her bike and moving.

her mother called. "Corry, did you look at the paper?"

"No, Ma. I never have time till after I deliver."

"Well, I think you've lost a customer. Isn't there a Mrs. Spector on your route?" her mother asked.

Corry shivered at the name. "Yeah, Ma. There's a Mrs. Spector. And you're right. I've lost a customer. I'm not going back there anymore. She's a very peculiar person."

"That's not what I mean. Look at the paper," Corry's mother said.

Corry came back down the stairs and took the paper from her mother. There was a large headline over the lead article.

**Woman Found Dead in
House on Claremont Street**

Police are investigating the mysterious death of Vera Spector, a young widow who lived alone at 562 Claremont Street. The body was discovered early this morning by the postman who called the sheriff's department. The coroner states that the woman had been dead at least two days. The cause of death has not yet been determined.